Books by Marcus Pfister

THE RAINBOW FISH*
RAINBOW FISH TO THE RESCUE*
THE RAINBOW FISH (board book)*
THE CHRISTMAS STAR*
DAZZLE THE DINOSAUR*
I SEE THE MOON
PENGIUN PETE*
PENGUIN PETE'S NEW FRIENDS*
PENGUIN PETE AND PAT
PENGUIN PETE, AHOY!
PENGUIN PETE AND LITTLE TIM
HOPPER*
HOPPER HUNTS FOR SPRING
HOPPER'S EASTER SURPRISE
HANG ON, HOPPER!
WAKE UP, SANTA CLAUS!

*also available in Spanish

Copyright © 1997 by Nord-Süd Verlag AG, Gossau Zürich, Switzerland
First published in Switzerland under the title *Hoppel weiss sich zu helfen.*
English translation copyright © 1997 by North-South Books Inc.
All rights reserved.
No part of this book may be reproduced or utilized in any form
or by any means, electronic or mechanical, including photocopying,
recording, or any information storage and retrieval system,
without permission in writing from the publisher.

First published in the United States, Great Britain, Canada,
Australia, and New Zealand in 1997 by North-South Books,
an imprint of Nord-Süd Verlag AG, Gossau Zürich, Switzerland.
Distributed in the United States by North-South Books Inc., New York.

Library of Congress Cataloging-in-Publication Data is available.
A CIP catalogue record for this book is available from The British Library.
ISBN 1-55858-680-6 (trade binding)
1 3 5 7 9 TB 10 8 6 4 2
ISBN 1-55858-681-4 (library binding)
1 3 5 7 9 LB 10 8 6 4 2
Printed in Belgium

For more information about our books, and the authors and artists
who create them, visit our web site: http://www.northsouth.com

Hopper's
Treetop Adventure

By Marcus Pfister

TRANSLATED BY ROSEMARY LANNING

North-South Books / New York / London

"Mama, may I go out on my own today?" said Hopper, one bright spring morning. "I want to find something good to eat."

"Where will you go?" his mother asked.

"Into the forest, to look for hazelnuts. I'm bored with bark and leaves."

His mother smiled. "You won't find hazelnuts in spring," she said. "Besides, hares don't usually eat nuts."

"Why not?" asked Hopper

"I suppose it's because we can't climb trees," said his mother.

Hopper ran across the fields and into the forest. The warmth of spring had melted the snow and ice from the trees, and washed it from the forest floor. That looked like a good place to explore. Suddenly, something hit him on the head. "Ouch!" cried Hopper. He stared up into the tree above him. More pine cones came hurtling down on Hopper.

An angry squirrel was glaring at him from the lowest branch of the tree. "Go away!" he shouted. "I won't let you steal my nuts!"

"Nuts?" said Hopper scornfully. "There are no nuts in spring. My mama said so."

"Well, there would be some if I could remember where I buried my winter stores," said the squirrel.

"I'll help you look," said Hopper. "If you'll share them with me."

"All right," said the squirrel, and they both began to dig around the tree.

"Look! I've found one!" said Hopper.

Then the squirrel found some more. "Let's go somewhere safe to eat these," he said. He picked up the nuts and scampered up into the tree.

"Wait! I can't climb trees," said Hopper.

"Maybe you could if you tried," said the squirrel.

"Will you help me?" asked Hopper.

The squirrel set the nuts in a hole in the tree. Then he helped Hopper drag a fallen branch over to the tree and prop it against the trunk. Hopper crawled slowly up the branch, not daring to look down. The squirrel was waiting at the top, and he helped Hopper onto the lowest branch of the tree.

"That was the hard part," said the squirrel. "The rest is easy. Just leap from branch to branch, like this!"

It did look easy and Hopper was good at jumping. But he was bigger and heavier than the squirrel, and landing on the narrow, slippery branches with his big, soft paws was a lot harder than it looked.

"Help!" cried Hopper suddenly. "I'm going to fall!"

"You'll be fine," said the squirrel calmly. "Just lower yourself onto this branch."

"Let's stop now," said Hopper, still trembling. "It's so high up here!"

The squirrel brought a nut for each of them, and showed Hopper how to crack open the shell with his teeth.

Hopper felt better now. "What's that tapping noise?" he asked.

"Oh, that's my friend the woodpecker," said the squirrel. "He lives in this tree too. Shall we visit him?"

"Hello, little hare," said the woodpecker. "How did you get up here?"

Hopper proudly explained how he had done it.

"Come inside and see my home," said the woodpecker.

Hopper and the squirrel crawled inside the hollow in the tree.

"This is a very nice place to live," said the squirrel.

"Yes, and it has a lovely view," said Hopper. "I'd like to stay longer, but I have to go home now."

Hopper managed to scramble down to the lowest branch, but the branch he had propped against the tree had fallen into the undergrowth.

"Now I'm stuck," he groaned.

"It *is* a long way to jump," the squirrel agreed.

"I know!" said Hopper, suddenly cheering up. "My friend the stag lives in this forest. Maybe he could lift me down."

"Good idea," said the woodpecker. "Wait here. I'll see if I can find him." And off he flew.

Soon they heard twigs crackling, and a big stag walked into the clearing.

"I see you need help," he said, and he held his antlers up to Hopper.

Hopper carefully climbed onto the antlers. Then the stag lowered his head and gently set Hopper down on the forest floor.

"Thank you," said Hopper. "I don't know how I would have managed without you."

"May I take a hazelnut home with me?" Hopper asked the squirrel.

"Of course," he replied. "I have plenty to spare."

Then the little hare said good-bye to his friends and set off for home.

"Did you find something good to eat?" asked Hopper's mother.

"Yes. And you'll never guess what it was," said Hopper.

He brought the hazelnut out from behind his back. "See, Mama? You *can* find hazelnuts in spring," said Hopper proudly. "And hares *can* climb trees—but I don't think I'll do it again. It was too scary."

His mother smiled. "It seems we both learned something today."

Then Hopper and his mother snuggled down in the grass and shared the springtime hazelnut.